GIRL IN THE TREE

Written by Ryan J. Tressel
Illustrations by Kristin Texeira

Text Copyright 2008-2010 Ryan J. Tressel
Artwork Copyright 2008-2010 Kristin Texeira

All rights reserved.
Published in the United States by James Jr. Press

This is a work of fiction. Any resemblance to any actual persons, living or dead, is entirely coincidental.

JAMES JR ISBN: 1453817670

www.ryantressel.com
www.kristintexeira.com

This book is dedicated to
Jeff Kent

Table of Contents

ABOUT (1)

The first question people always ask you is "What is it about?" This proved to be the most difficult part of releasing my first novel 'The While' last year. "What is it about?" I didn't really have an answer, at least not one I was ever comfortable with.

When I was entering high school, I spent two summers at an advanced studies program hosted at a local college. 500 or so boys and girls spent six weeks in a college dorm, taking what purported to be college level classes, and stewed in our own hormonal juices. Both summers I took the same class: Creative Writing, taught by a local high school English teacher named Jeff Kent. And each summer, in addition to the dozens of poems and smaller personal narratives we were assigned, we were asked by Jeff Kent to write a short story. He loved the story I wrote that first summer. The one from the second summer, he hated.

So your next question might likely be: "What were they about?" (It also might be "Why did he love one and hate the other?" which is kind of just a different way of asking the same thing.) That's easier with the second story. It was about a suicidal clown, deciding the moment after he jumps off the building that he no longer wants to die. He spends the entire story trying to pull himself up while a series of hilarious mishaps plague him. A crowd gathers below and mistakes it for some kind of performance. This was the one he hated.

The first story, the one Jeff Kent loved, was about a man who, while grocery shopping, stumbles upon an elderly woman threatening the cashier with a pearl-handled pistol over a Vanilla wafers coupon discrepancy. The man, who is unnamed, pushes his carriage out of the store and out into the parking lot and continues down the street, finally stopping at a brook at the edge of town. The elderly woman follows him the whole time, threatening him with the gun, telling him to stop. She, too, stops at the brook, and tells the man her life story before lying down and dying. Then the man pushes the carriage back to the grocery store.

I spent two summers as a youth with Jeff Kent, and wrote two stories for him. I couldn't really understand why he so preferred the first story, which I thought was kind of meandering and pointless, to the second. But then, as summer camps with teenagers often allow, I met a girl, and then the opinions of my creative writing teacher became suddenly less important. Jeff Kent presented me with an award on the last day of the program, shook my hand, and told me to keep on writing. I was polite to him, but I'm sure I rushed off to go pledge undying love to a girl somewhere.

Then I grew up, in a manner. I graduated from high school, went to college, and wrote an awful lot. Ten years after I was a student at the summer program, I was hired to be an intern there, and I became Jeff Kent's assistant. He remembered my first story--really concrete details about a story he hadn't read in a decade. He didn't remember the second story at all. At least not that he mentioned to me.

So I guess the point is that people sometimes mean two different things when they ask what a story is about. Most of the time, I think, they mean, "What is the plot?" Less often, they want to know what the story is about. The second story, about the clown, was about humiliation. The first one--the one about the grocery cart--(and this is probably hard to believe without having read the story, and believe me, I'm not about to go and air that dirty laundry.) The first story was about loneliness. About kindness. When they are sitting together on the brook, the old woman tells the young man that she used to beautiful. That she had grown old, had buried her husband and her son. The younger man kisses her, and she thanks him. The story was about grace.

Jeff Kent retired shortly thereafter, and recommended me to replace him. He had been working at the program for nearly its entire 40-year history, and was their longest serving master teacher, so I was both extraordinarily touched and daunted by his gesture. I took over the class and was initially frustrated by the number of really talented young writers who, for whatever reason, felt the need to write stories about wizards and dragons (that was mainly the boys) or vampires and werewolves (primarily the girls). They would spend all their time developing worlds that would need an entire novel to explore, and trying to do so in four-five page stories.

I'm far from the first person to say this, and I won't pretend that what I'm saying is in any way profound, but I think the moment of true writing adulthood is realizing that writing about what happens is not nearly as interesting or rewarding as writing about who it happens to.

Right before my second summer as the summer program's creative writing master teacher, I lost my fulltime teaching job at the local high school I'd been working at for the past few years. I was pretty uncertain what I was going to do come that September, when the summer program ended and the new school year started, but at some point I decided I would try to become a writer again. I hadn't written anything in a number of years, so that meant I would have to learn how to be a writer again. I set myself a goal of writing one short story a week, and I stuck to it, starting in the end of August and finishing in the early days of October. I had written these stories as a warm up to the novel I ended up writing between October and December of 2008, "The While." I'm not going to make any great claims about these stories--some of them work better than others, some are more character sketches than stories. I'll let the reader decide for themselves how to classify them. What's is important to me is that they gave me the confidence I needed to embark on a longer project. And enough of them were interesting enough to me to decide to share them.

I'm grateful to Jeff Kent for giving me the opportunity: to be his student, his apprentice, and his replacement. Each one of those roles have been extraordinarily important to my life as a writer, and as a reader. I don't know how many of these stories he would like. Maybe a couple. Maybe none.

What are they about?
What are all stories about?
They're about me.

-Ryan J. Tressel
Somewhere on the Back River
December 2009.

MY NAME IS JASON

Although it still takes me a second to respond to it. It's kind of hard to explain, but for about six years my name was something else. It's not like a witness protection thing or anything. It's just complicated.

My older brother Bobby died when I was fourteen in kind of a horrific motorcycle accident. For a while, I told people I was with him when it happened, that I was thrown clear, that I broke my arm and my right femur, but I still crawled to him and was beside him when he died. I was actually at Boy Scout camp at the time, and I didn't find out until the day after it happened and my uncle came to pick me up. "Bobby's dead," he told me matter-of-factly, although my therapist thinks I'm making that part up, too, and that he probably put it a lot more delicately.

About six months after that, I started to think I was my brother. It started in early September. Bobby had been the star running back on our high school football team and I think he still holds the record for running yards, but I haven't checked in seven or eight years. Before school started I went into the football coach's office and told him that I'd take my brother's place on the team. I hadn't even started my freshmen year yet, and I'd never played football before. I'd only played one season of youth soccer before I quit. The coach hardly played me because I'd drift off during the games. But I told the football coach, who I knew from some of the pasta fests my mom would have for the team, and also from Bobby's wake and funeral, where he showed up wearing a black jacket over a white polo. I don't remember the coach's name.

I don't know why I just said that. His name was John Lindsay and I had him my junior year for Standard English.

We called him Mr. L. So I went into Mr. L's office and said that I could take Bobby's position on the starting line-up. I even said I'd wear Bobby's jersey, which Mr. L had already ordered with our last name on the back. "We have the same last name," I said to Mr. L. "You wouldn't have to order me a new one."

"I know, son," he said. He told me when try-outs were, and even though I didn't show up, he asked me to be part of the team anyway, and I spent a lot of time getting water and carrying equipment. All of the guys on the team were real nice to me, and they all had my brother's number sewn onto their jerseys. I know it made my dad real proud. My mom never went to any of the games.

It wasn't until after Christmas, sometime in January, I think, that I started telling people my name was Robert. "But you can call me Bobby," I'd say. I think I started doing it first to people who I hadn't met before. We lived right on the town line, so sometimes I'd walk to the next town, just go to the convenience stores and pharmacies and stuff. "Hi, my name is Bobby." Nobody seemed to care. Most people don't introduce themselves to you when they're buying Jolly Ranchers.

I did it once in the grocery store with my mom. I just wasn't thinking and I told the older woman ringing us up that my name was Robert. Her name tag said "Roberta" and I think I said "Hey, we've got the same name" or something. My mother either didn't notice or just didn't say anything.

Then one day I just stopped answering to Jason. And then I stopped thinking I was Jason. I started calling Bobby's old girlfriend Brittany and the first couple of times she was really nice about it, but I got the sense she might be seeing someone else and I got real nasty about it one night. She sounded like she was crying. "Jason, this isn't funny," she said. "Stop calling me." And then she hung up.

When I saw her at school the next day, I kind of got in her face. "How could you do this to me?" "I love you!" Stuff like that. I was still a freshmen, and like a buck twenty-five, and she was a senior and her new boyfriend, or the new guy she was seeing, he kind of shoved me up against the lockers and told me to back off. His name was Wes. I actually saw him at the bar the other night and he patted me on the back and asked me how things were going. He called me "Buddy" which I think means he couldn't remember my name, which is probably best.

Shortly after that, my parents pulled me from school. My brother's death had really affected me and it would be better if I took some time and started fresh in the fall. The school arranged for a home tutor but he only came in the afternoons since both my parents worked and the school had a rule about making sure the tutor was never alone with the student. So I spent all day, most days by myself. I'd go into my brother's old room and dress up in his clothes. They were always too big for me, but I rolled up the cuffs of the pants. A few times I would fall asleep on top of my bed, just wearing his clothes, and I would kind of masturbate through the pants. Eventually my parents put a padlock on his door.

Sometime that summer they sent me to a therapist. The first one I had, just kept asking me what I thought about my brother. Like over and over again. I mean, he'd ask different questions all the time, but they were all basically the same. "What do you think about your brother?" I think that's when I started telling people that I was on the motorcycle with him.

The following year I went to a private school, someplace

where nobody knew who I was. I think my parents had a meeting with the principal and the school psychologist, because once I started going there, everybody called me Bobby. It was no big thing. But on the roll in each class the first day, it was always 'Robert' not 'Jason.'

And things got better and I made some friends. I even met a girl named Daphne who I was kind of serious with for a while. I brought her home a couple of times, but my mother really disliked her. I heard her say the word 'slut' to my father. But Daphne and I never did it. She let me finger her once. She kept cooing softly "Oh, Bobby" while I did it and I came in my pants, even though she didn't touch me even once. We broke up like a week later, although she said it wasn't really breaking up because we were never really going out. I went to her house once and tried to get her to take me back. Her father had a really bad moustache. He stood at the door and wouldn't let me in. I think I might've been crying. "Stop making a scene, Robert," he said. "I think it's time you went home." So I did.

It was weird that I thought I was my brother, but it became so normal, too. After the thing with Daphne's dad, I didn't really want to be called Bobby anymore but too many people thought it was my real name. I thought about going back to my old school but my dad said they'd spent too much money sending me to private school for me to throw it all away and my mother said everybody at my old school thought I was crazy. "Do you think I'm crazy?" I asked her.

Her eyes were all red and her lips were quivering a bit. "End of discussion." And it was.

I should note at this point that my parents never called me Robert or Bobby. But they didn't call me Jason, either. My father called me either son or buddy. And my mother stopped calling me anything at all.

So I finished high school and thought maybe I'd go back to being Jason once I got back to college, but my friend Will decided to go to the same school as me, and we ended up being roommates. He started smoking a lot of pot and ended up flunking out second semester. But by that point I was already known everywhere as Bob or Bobby, so there was nothing I could really do.

My sophomore year I met Megan in my Psych class. She had the prettiest eyes and kind of crazy freckles and she had really black hair. She was really really skinny and I would sometimes catch myself staring at her bones when she wore tighter shirts and stuff. I couldn't get enough of those shoulder blades.

We started hanging out a lot, walking after class, and I usually would miss my next class because Megan didn't have a class after Psych and I'd just keep talking to her in the parking lot. We started dating after Christmas break. She was the first girl I slept with. I still remember the first time we made love; she was like a little bird, all soft noises and tiny bones. I remember I could see her heartbeat kind of flutter under her skin. Afterwards, she traced her fingernails across my chest, like she spelling things out. I wanted to ask her to stop, because her nails kind of hurt, but I didn't. I've always had very sensitive skin.

She caught me lying a few times, small things, no big deal. Like I bought a paper for my International Relations class from some guy online and I don't remember how she found out, but she wasn't too happy. And another time I told her I got Dave Matthews tickets even though I hadn't, figuring… but they sold out. Otherwise we had our stupid fights like everybody, I guess and it turned out she lived forty minutes from my parents' house so we could still see each other over the summer.

Except I kind of made out with this girl at a party back home. And then we went out a couple of times. She was kind of overweight, and I don't know what I was thinking, because her breath always smelled bad, too. And it looked like she might've had to shave her face, because she had kind of hairy arms and weird bumps on her neck. But she was kind of funny and she had really nice blonde hair that smelled like oranges.

I don't remember the details, so don't ask me, but they were stupid. It might've been on IM or something, but somehow when we got back to school, Megan found out about the girl from the summer, who really liked me, I guess and Megan was pissed. I wasn't the first guy she'd slept with, but I think I was the first guy she loved, and she got really hurt and wouldn't talk to me.

I went to her dorm and just cried and cried because I thought she would see I was so sorry and I also because I was really upset and that's how I handled things back in those days.

She yelled and called me a lot of things. A lot of nasty names. She said I'd really hurt her, and she kind of knew deep down I always would.

It didn't seem like she was going to forgive me and take me back, so I pulled out the big guns. I told her the whole story about my brother dying in a motorcycle accident and how it had fucked me up for so long and it had been five years and I still wasn't over it. "My name's not even Bobby," I said, sobbing. "My name is Jason."

She looked at me a long time and just kind of kept crunching up her face, like she was having a hard time seeing me, like I was out of focus or something. Finally, she just looked at me and said, "I don't believe you." I never talked to her again after that night. I went home at the end of the fall semester for Christmas break and decided not to go back. Dad had moved out by that point so it was just me and Mom, and once she saw my grades, I don't think she wanted me to go back, either.

I got a job at Radio Shack, and when I applied, I put Jason on the application, and the manager really liked me, even thought he'd get mad when he'd call my name and I wouldn't answer him. It took me a while to get used to it.

I'm still in therapy. My third therapist was the one I stuck with. I really like her. She doesn't ask me a whole lot of questions, she just kind of lets me talk. A few months ago, she asked me a question. She asked me what was my strongest memory of my brother.

I said he was like everybody's older brother, because he was cool and cruel and I wanted to be just like him and I hated him, too. I wasn't good at sports, so we didn't play outside together a lot. And he always seemed to have a lot of friends to hang out with, and I liked playing on the computer and I was really into fantasy when he died. I hadn't read one since he died, although I did pick a few up at Borders with the gift certificate Dad sent me for my birthday.

But she wanted a memory, a specific one, and all I could think of was this time Mom and Dad had taken us up to Maine for a camping trip--I think it was the last time Bobby had come with us--and on the way home me and him and Dad just quoted from different movies we liked. And it drove my mom nuts. And then, probably because of the Burger King we had, we just started farting. Just really stinking up the car.

Even my dad got kind of mad, but we couldn't help it. So me and Bobby just kept farting and laughing and laughing and farting and trying to wave our farts to the front of the car. I cried so hard that session, just thinking about it.

That night I went home and wrote Megan an email, saying I was sorry. She sent me a nice reply and sent me pictures of her niece, who had been born the week before.

So now it's just me and mom and about a month ago I bought a dog, a golden retriever. I named him Gus, and on my days off from work, I walk him to the park near our house. There's a little manmade pond there, and I let Gus off his leash and let him go into the pond. I sit on the picnic table and trace my name with my fingernail on the table and I watch him as he wades out into the water getting just far enough that his head stays above water but his feet can't touch the ground, so he turns around and paddles his way back and shakes off all the water.

And then we walk back home.

CIVICS

Lauren Campbell hasn't thrown up since September 11th.

At first I think she's making some kind of proud declaration against bulimia, because it's only the 14th. I'm halfway through thinking this when I hear her talking about the Twin Towers, and I realize she isn't filling us in on her battle with an eating disorder, but instead equating the constitutional fortitude of her stomach lining with the safety and security of the USA.

I guess her vomit is supposed to be all of our vomit, and we're supposed to respect her ability to not choke up the gross food they serve us here as her contribution to the War on Terror.

Mr. Friedman keeps letting her talk, doing that thing with his tongue across his teeth under his lips that I know he thinks we don't notice, even though he does it everyday we have Civics right after lunch. So even though Lauren Campbell is still talking about President Bush and I know I really should be listening to it, if only to quote back what she says to her to show her how little she understands global politics, all I can think about is: what is in Mr. Friedman's teeth that drives him so compulsively to run his tongue across them? What does he have for lunch--something with sesame seeds perhaps? And before I realize it I'm thinking when was the last time Mr. Friedman threw up and now I'm thinking when was the last time Mr. Friedman had sex?

And suddenly I'm doing that thing where I'm wondering whether everybody in the room has had sex yet. And while I'm thinking about it, I can't help trying to picture each person in the room having sex, and wondering why it is I can never picture anyone having sex despite having seen that part in Inventing the Abbots where Jennifer Connolly has sex with the brother that isn't Joaquin Phoenix. I know what sex looks like, even through my mother tried to fast forward through that part, because by the time she found the remote it was over and she had inadvertently fast forwarded through the next scene, and refused to rewind it back so we could see what we missed.

The point being, no matter how I try, I can't picture Lauren Campbell having sex, even though I'm pretty sure she has, because she's been going out with Tom Russo for a year and a half. But whenever I try, all I can see is her wearing the oversized "United We Stand" t-shirt she wore that day in Middle School they dragged us outside to sing "God Bless the USA." Or "America the Beautiful." Yeah, it was "American the Beautiful."

Lauren Campbell is still talking about supporting our president during war, surprisingly--well, surprising she's still talking, not that she's talking about supporting President Bush, but Mr. Friedman's still cleaning his teeth and nodding every once and a while, which means he's probably not really listening.

But the Friday after September 11th--the Friday after the last time Lauren Campbell threw up apparently--the school had "Patriotic Day" and sent a letter home to our parents asking them to dress us up in Red, White, and Blue clothes and they had us all stand in the courtyard and recite the Pledge of Allegiance, and sing "America the Beautiful" and stuff. My mom of course forgot, so I was wearing my favorite green and purple polka dot dress, and I remember Mrs. Waters making me call home to get a change of clothes because someone from the paper was coming to take a picture, but because my mom's a nurse and my dad wasn't living in the state at the time, I pretended to call home, but really just sat and listened to the dial tone on the office phone for a minute before saying that no one was home, so Mrs. Waters told me I'd have to stand in the back.

And Lauren Campbell was wearing this ridiculously large t-shirt that said "United We Stand" that came down to her knees and I remember thinking they should put her in the back because her shirt was so big it looked like she didn't have any pants on. But I guess it's more important to look Patriotic than to look like you know how to dress yourself.

And it's then I realize that it's like her misconceptions are so big that it makes her ideas look like they're not wearing any pants, and I kind of half-laugh, and she stops talking for a second and she kind of leers at me and says "What? Do you disagree or something, Mona?" And of course I do, because she's kind of an idiot, but I wasn't listening to what she was just saying, and I almost say the thing about her ideas looking pants-less, but I realize nobody would know what I was talking about. So I just kind of sit there for a second, until Warren Jacobs pipes up and says, "A lot of us disagree, Lauren." He looks at me and continues, "A lot of us think that Bush is the worst president we ever had."

And then I realize that I'm in love with Warren Jacobs.

Which is weird, because I've never really even liked him before, especially because one time he copied off my Earth Science test and actually got a higher grade than me. But that was before I heard him say things like "Bush is like Hitler" and "This administration doesn't care about you or your safety. They only care about oil." Which is true.

Mr. Friedman has stopped licking his teeth and tells Warren to take it easy, which is just like Mr. Friedman, because he hates when people criticize President Bush, although now that I think about it, he does have an old Kerry bumper sticker on his car. It's a Mazda Miata, I don't know the year, but I do know that it's blue, and that's only because I saw him leaving school one day while I was waiting for my mom to come pick me up.

But Warren keeps going, and then when Lauren tries to argue back, he tells her to stop being such a naïve idiot and to stop being a parrot for what the government wants her to think. Then Lauren starts crying and screams that her cousin is over in Iraq and then Warren just kind of stops and is slack-jawed.

And I want him to jump up and say that because you have a cousin in Iraq means you should be even more critical of the government because the president has sent him into harm's way for no good reason, based on a lie, and that it's the job of a citizenry to always be vigilant and question its leaders, because that's what democracies are all about.

And then I imagine Warren and I joining the Debate Team and becoming state champions, even though our school doesn't even have a debate team, in fact I don't think I've ever heard of a debate team existing outside of a movie, but we win the state championship and Mr. Friedman will take the team out to dinner at Chili's to celebrate our victory and Warren I will be sitting outside on the benches while everybody will be ordering dessert, and he'll tell me I did a great job defending the President of Venezuela and he'll kiss me and then we'll go to the Prom and win King and Queen. We'll dance to "We've Got Tonight," a song which I hate normally, but which I wouldn't mind in the context of a prom.

But then Warren just says, "I'm sorry. Obviously, I support our troops over in Iraq." I wait for his retort, his but one can oppose the President's policies while still supporting our troops…but he doesn't. He realizes now that the class has turned against him, and Mr. Friedman gives him another second to continue, but Warren just kind of looks down at his desk, and then Mr. Friedman looks around the room and says, "Anyone else?"

I think about telling the class about being forced to stand in the back during Patriotic Day for wearing green polka dots, which is actually more Patriotic, if you ask me, because it means the terrorists didn't make me change what I was going to wear. And how when we were supposed to be singing "America the Beautiful," I looked over at Mr. Phillips' class at my friend Angela, and Angela was doing that thing where she's staring off into space, but you know she's thinking about something about something about a million times more interesting and ingenious than you've ever thought about, and then Mr. Phillips kind of grabbed her arm and snapped at her because she wasn't singing, and how she looked when he did it, like he ripped her out of a peaceful, happy place and she was so scared to be back in a world where terrorists fly planes into buildings and authority figures yell at you for not singing songs that they want you to sing.

But I notice that the period is almost over and I don't want to start talking about something and have the bell ring because if someone is talking when the bell rings, Mr. Friedman makes everyone stay seated until they've finished talking, and then everyone just looks at you, waiting for you to finish, so you feel self-conscious and just kind of hurry and wrap everything up so people won't be late to their next class.

"No?" Mr. Friedman asks. And then he waits a second and says "Okay" and then assigns the nightly reading.

After class, I go to my locker, and I can see Warren chase after Lauren and tell her he's very sorry about her cousin and how he never would've said anything if he'd known and that he respects and honors her cousin's service.

What a tool. I think he just said those things to impress Mr. Friedman or maybe Tori because she said some anti-Bush things last week and I know he has a crush on her because he is always at the Girls' Track meets (I'm the manager) and he is always telling her she had a good meet, even though she almost never does. I mean, she's nice enough, and Lord knows her boobs are like quadruple D's, but you'd think Warren would have better taste than that.

I put my Civics book in my locker and as I watch him skulk away from Lauren Campbell who looks like she might throw up she's so upset, except that I know she's holding back the vomit because otherwise the terrorists will win, and I can't believe I actually thought I liked him. I've never really liked him, because in sixth grade he wouldn't dance with me at the Holiday dance, saying he didn't want to dance with anybody, although he did dance with Sarah Cook like two songs later. I guess it's easy to fall in love with your idea of a person. Maybe it's better that way, because all people will do in real life is disappoint you.

And that's what I learned in Civics class today.

THE BIG CAT

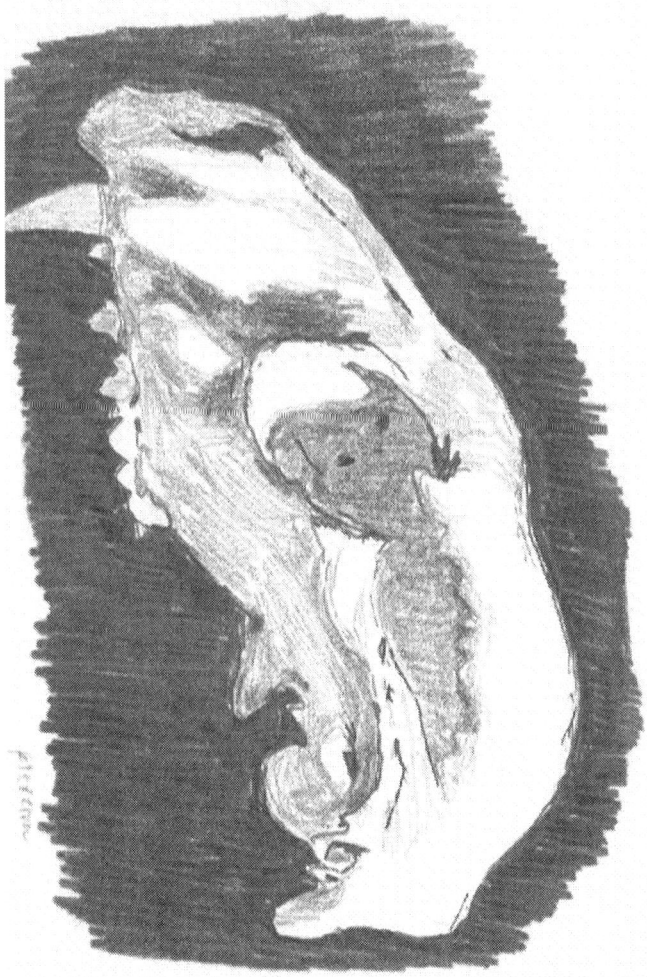

Dream of running. Dark and bright and colors and legs springing. Pumpkin chase, happy running. No wind, still air, Pumpkin dreaming. No chase. No wake. Sun is warm by window. Pumpkin sleeps in warm. Wake sharp, quick, no chase. Now wake.

Once window open, Pumpkin feel air move, chase moths and little things that dance against screen. Bat at with claws out, tear screen, make She mad. Warm air gone, window closed, no moths little things against screen. Nothing to claw.

So Pumpkin sit in warm. Glass makes shine light warm, air cold outside. Pumpkin's fur is thick now. Cold is here.

Pumpkin stretch legs. She comes and touches Pumpkin. Pumpkin bone so close to skin. Pumpkin old. Pumpkin tired. She hands feel nice, soft, warm. Pumpkin purr.

Pumpkin dream again. Sleep easy now. Dark easy now. Night eyes see better, dream eyes see better. There things to chase in dream. Pumpkin run in dream. Wake Pumpkin run no more. Old. Tired. Bone close to skin. No run no more.

Wake by scent, strong. Pumpkin have no wake dream to tell what scent is. Inside is not. Scent is outside. Pumpkin smell whole inside along the hard part, hard bottom and hard sides. Scent outside. Scent bad.

Inside meets outside, Pumpkin there. She needs to come, open inside to outside. She not come. She sit, watch She dreams outside of She head. She dreams make noise Pumpkin hear. Lights, too. Pumpkin cries at the inside outside. Pumpkin cries so She comes. She comes not. She noises kisses. She noises Pumpkin come to She sit. Pumpkin out. Understand She? Pumpkin out. Pumpkin cry. Out. Out. Out. Out. Scent out. Pumpkin out.

{30}

She here. Look Pumpkin, noise Pumpkin. No out Pumpkin, She noise. Must out. Must out. No pumpkin, She noise.

Pumpkin love She. Pumpkin make know. Pumpkin love She with head. Rub feels nice. Rub show love. Pumpkin love. But Pumpkin out. Pumpkin love, but Pumpkin go. Scent strong. Pumpkin go.

She smalls down to Pumpkin. She rub face and head and Pumpkin tail start where Pumpkin claws cannot go. Nice. Touch nice She. Pumpkin out, though. Pumpkin out. Love now, no love after. Pumpkin out, Pumpkin gone.

Pumpkin cry. She make inside outside. Air moves now. Cold. She noise Pumpkin. She noise Why no out Pumpkin, all that crying? Pumpkin fear, Pumpkin scent fear. Pumpkin miss She, will. No more Pumpkin. Pumpkin out, no again in. Pumpkin say goodbye. Love She. Goodbye, She.

Inside now outside. She makes inside closed. Pumpkin see She in window. Cold air moving, scent strong bad fear, Pumpkin inside? No. No more inside again. Pumpkin out now.

Ground, grass, cold, hard. In the warm, grass soft, ground soft. Now cold, hard. Air moves cold fast against fur. Pumpkin scent own. Mix with bad scent. Must clean Pumpkin. Must make no scent. Tongue clean Pumpkin. Wash away Pumpkin scent. Make Pumpkin invisible. Must hunt bad scent.

No up life. No uplife songs or taunting Pumpkin. Uplife fly away with warm. Only groundlife now, in cold. Scent is strong. Groundlife must be near. Pumpkin smell air move. Follow air move, follow scent. Must be big. Pumpkin no hunger, but Pumpkin hunt big smell. Pumpkin hunt big smell, bring big smell home, show She Pumpkin love. No. No Pumpkin home. No Pumpkin show love. Pumpkin out now.

Dead brown crunch ground. Smell like old sky. Pumpkin

paws crunch dead brown, noise, bad noise. Bad noise for hunt. Pumpkin slow. Pumpkin paws slow. Make little noise. Bad smell bigger. Pumpkin not close. Pumpkin needs further. Further into outside. Outside bigger than before. Pumpkin know outside, not know this outside. Pumpkin bones tired, closer to skin. Pumpkin sleep, dream of chase? No. No sleep. Chase in wake. Chase in now. Hunt in now. Big smell. Big smell hunt.

Air move hurt. Cold hurt. Air noise, crying. Move Pumpkin, push Pumpkin, hard like inside. Pumpkin push back. Cold, hard. Pumpkin need move on. Pumpkin hunt big smell. Pumpkin find more outside. New outside, far from inside. Pumpkin hunts.

Pumpkin wake dreams about kin. Tiny, small Pumpkin, before Pumpkin. Brothersisters suckle mother's milk. Warm, sweet. Pumpkin and brothersisters squeeze to reach teat. No know then life. Know then only milk, warm. No love. Mother knew love. Cleaned Pumpkin, protected Pumpkin from big things.

Why Pumpkin wake dream this? Old things in Pumpkin wake dream now. Wake dream She, holding Pumpkin giving Pumpkin name. Fur so soft, Pumpkin so little. She Pumpkin carry. She new mother. Milk pool, now. No teat. She hairless paws, rub head, say Pumpkin Pumpkin Pumpkin Pumpkin until know. Know Pumpkin. Am Pumpkin.

Bad scent strong. Outside now everything. No inside anymore. Pumpkin stop wake dream. Look up. Bad scent here. Big Cat here.

Hello Small Cat, Big Cat mew. Big Cat fear make Pumpkin, scare. Pumpkin hiss, arch back, try make fear Big Cat. No skin. Bone, claw, teeth. Big Cat no fear.

No hiss, Small Cat. No fight. Time, Small Cat, time.

No Small Cat. Pumpkin, no Small Cat. Big Cat shakes head. Pumpkin is She name. Before you suckle teat, you no Pumpkin. All are Small Cat to Big Cat.

Pumpkin fear. Big Cat say No fear, no fear. Pumpkin inside now Pumpkin outside. Understand?

Pumpkin hiss more. Bad big scent. Big Cat bad. Small cat, you go outside now. Sleep no dream. Sleep now on.

Pumpkin tired. Pumpkin lie on brown cold. Pumpkin cold. Pumpkin wake dream little groundlife and uplife. Fear make, play with little life, ground and up, play and make fear. Pumpkin sorry, Little Life, for fear. Pumpkin not know how fear Big Cat is. Pumpkin fear now, so Pumpkin sorry.

Be not sorry, Small Cat. How made Small Cat. Not fault. How made.

No more love, Big Cat? No more warm and windows and food in dish, given by She paws? No more chasing light around inside, and warming against She? No more love?

Big Cat loves you, Small Cat. Not like She loves. Different, but love.

Why, Big Cat? Pumpkin hunt, Pumpkin love, Pumpkin fear. Pumpkin alone. Why Pumpkin alone?

Small Cat, you are not alone. Never alone. No scared. How made. Made to live and run and chase, now made to lie. No scared.

Lay down, Small Cat. Lay down. Think about inside. Now there are little things inside Small Cat. Little things are hungry. Small Cat will make them happy, make them full. Cold ground will be warm again. Small Cat you will make warm ground grow again. It all love, from Mother's teat to She paws to the little things inside you to the ground you make warm. All love. Lay down.

Sleep. Pumpkin sleep. Dark, no colors, no light. Just sleep
All love. Understand. Pumpkin understand. Now.

PLENTY OF TIME

They were making love in the break room of the Safeway after hours when he first heard God speak to him. He had discovered that sex in risky situations excited her, and since he was an assistant manager he knew he had until one a.m. to set the alarm before someone from the security company would call his boss, and that seemed like plenty of time. But once-- later, the next morning,--he realized that it truly was God who had spoken to him, he realized that there was never going to be enough time--not to atone for all the sinful things he had done in his life.

He walked down to the pond behind his parents' house with a pad and a pen and he tried to make a list: he had sworn and lied and stole (small things, inconsequential; but he felt that such matters of degree were immaterial) he had shot at squirrels with his air rifle, thrown rocks at frogs, and had been sinful with women--so many women. Especially if he counted all the girls who he had kissed or fondled, which for his pur-poses, he did.

So he called his girlfriend that evening and told her he needed some time to think. He meant it, too, because next he went to the Safeway and told his manager about his disgusting abuse of the break room. The manager had no choice but to fire him. But it was God's will.

"What did God say to you?" his mother asked. He said he wasn't sure, but he knew that He had. He didn't tell her about the break room.

He took down all the posters in his room, even the ones that didn't seem blasphemous, like his Manny Ramirez poster. He spent time tracing the areas where the posters had been, where the paint was more vibrant, less faded. "This is what my soul is like," he thought.

He had met born-again Christians before, and he had always found them rude and judgmental. He knew he didn't want to be like that, so when he told his friends he wasn't going to drink or smoke anymore, he said it was for health reasons, which he figured wasn't really a lie. He called his girlfriend again and told her that he still had strong feelings for her, but he still needed time.

His parents had never been very religious, so they asked their friends for advice. The neighbors down the street were Catholics and they said the priest in their parish was young and funny and really related well to young people. They also made a point to stress that he wasn't anyone that they should worry about with their son. This made them feel better, although they were kind of ashamed to admit to each other that they felt that way.

So they contacted the priest and made an appointment for him to meet their son. He came to their house, driving up in a blue Volkswagon. He was wearing sunglasses, which was surprising, but given the brightness of the mid-morning summer sun, it shouldn't have been. The priest sat down in the living room in the father's chair, and the son pulled a chair in from the kitchen. They sat across from one another and spoke mainly about pleasantries and small conversational matters. After an hour, the mother asked the priest if he needed a drink. He asked if they had any club soda, which struck the son as an odd thing to ask. Aren't there more important questions?

When the mother went back into the other room, the priest turned to the boy and asked, "Hey, you guys validate parking here, right?" The boy got nervous for a second, as he thought the priest had parked in the driveway, and then the priest smiled and said, "Relax. I'm only kidding."

He had a big smile, and the boy liked how many of the priest's teeth he could see, especially the crooked ones on the bottom. They talked for a little bit longer and then the priest left. The boy sat in the kitchen chair in the living room silently for quite a while after, not really moving very much. The father asked him after about an hour if he was alright.

"I was just thinking," the son replied.

The girl came by later that night to return some books and Cds and movies he had left at her house. He told her that she could keep them, but she looked so upset. She didn't understand what had happened, and he wasn't about to tell her. He gave her a hug and told her that he still needed time. She looked either angry or frustrated or maybe just overtired. He told her he would talk to her soon. He promised, even. Then she got in her dad's Camry and drove off.

That night he made a new list. All the dirty thoughts he'd ever had about girls he had known. (He decided to leave off the ones about famous actresses and models.)

The next week he brought the list to the rectory and showed it to the priest. "I don't think Santa will be able to get all of these for you this year," the priest said, and then showed his crooked bottom teeth. "I'm teasing."

The boy took the list away from the priest and folded it back up into quarters and put it in his front shirt pocket.

"I feel like I have so many questions, but I don't know what they are," he said to the priest.

"Ah," the priest replied.

About a month later, a letter came in the mail from the girl, which the boy liked because it seemed so old-fashioned.

It said that she thought that he really loved her and that she wouldn't done those things with him if she knew he was just using her.

That night he sat down to write her a letter, in which he said that he thought that he might love her, and that he really missed her company and her smile, but that Jesus didn't want him to have sex until he was married, that it was hard to see her and not be reminded of the sinful things they had done together.

It was a humid and sticky night. So he stopped writing the letter and went for a run. When he got back home, covered in sweat and with aches still in his legs and his lungs, he decided he should make a list of all the sinful thoughts he had had about girls he knew, and by the time he realized he had already made a list like that, he was so close to finishing that he decided to just keep on going. He put the list with the unfinished letter and went to sleep.

Fall came, then winter, and the boy would bring the lists he made to the rectory, and the priest would glance at them and ask the boy if he planned to go back to college or if he planned to try and find a job. They were the same questions his father had been asking him. "Working and education are good for the soul," the priest said. The boy felt there was collusion going on. And then sometime late that winter, the priest was relocated to another Parish, in the western part of the state. It was a three hour drive, and the boy and the priest had never really talked about all that much that made sense to the boy. He had started smoking again, anyway, figuring that there didn't seem to be any rules against it anywhere.

He had never gone to church, and slowly and small at first, he stopped thinking a lot of the things he had been thinking, and even started to doubt that it was God's voice he heard while he had his pants around his ankles in the break room. But he felt like it must have been, and prayed each night for God to give him another sign. The next day he started to make lists of things that might possibly be signs from God. He wrote them down in a tiny notebook he had found in his basement, with Batman on the front. The first couple of pages were filled with lists he had made when he was nine--one was a list of boys in his grade who were his friends, another he had written down all the TV shows he liked and what nights they were on. He thought about ripping those pages out, but kept them in there.

Some of the possible signs from God included an old man holding hands with an old lady as the crossed the street, how blue the sky looked one cold Tuesday morning in early April, the sounds of robins in the trees outside his bedroom window, the pizzeria in the center of town's 99 cent pizza night.

One night while had been trying to think and had needed some space, the girl had fallen out of a second story window and landed head first. She was killed instantly. The papers initially mentioned something about alcohol, but subsequent articles didn't mention that, and when the boy went to the wake, the casket was closed, as if her head had met with the ground in some immediate and irreconcilable way.

Her funeral was a beautiful spring day, and the service was remarkably short. This priest was older, and seemed to have little to say about the girl at all. The boy, feeling he needed more than the standard funeral service provided, called his priest, and asked if he could come see him. The priest said certainly and gave him directions and never asked the boy what was the matter.

The boy cried most of the drive there. As he drove down the long highway, he saw Safeways every few exits, and other supermarkets, and pharmacies, and shopping plazas. He felt surprised and saddened by how large and expansive the state was. He had never traveled so far west, and he realized that he never knew how large, and how small, things really were.

As he drove he thought about his lists, the one he kept in his notebook, and how he didn't know if he should add this or not. He thought about what he would say to the priest when he got there. He had so many questions, and didn't know what they all were. A lot of them seemed questions that the priest would be ill-suited to answering. Why had he waited so long to call the girl back? How come he never finished that letter? What was so wrong about having sex in the break room of Safeway that he would make her feel so bad and alone and unloved about it? Why did bad things happen to good people?

He found the rectory a few miles off the highway, just like the priest had told him. There was a woman outside the rectory, carrying trash bags up to the rectory office from off the street. The boy offered to help. "I don't know why," the woman said, "but some weeks the garbage men don't pick up our trash. I'll have to put it behind the shed, but the raccoons and mice still get into it." The boy helped her carry the bags behind the shed. She thanked him and then led him to the priest's office. The door looked heavier, maybe made of a finer wood, than the priest's old door. The boy knocked.

The priest opened the door, and looked at his young friend and said, "It's been more than thirty minutes, young man. That pizza better be free." He extended his hand and smiled. "I'm only kidding," he said.

It seemed a long way to come for a joke.

GO BACK TO YOUR HOMES

All up and down Patterson, blue lights shunt into windows. It's the wives that wake up first, that stir and shuffle toward the window, clutching nightgowns across their chests. "Wake up, honey," they say to their sleeping husbands, dozing and farting into the violently blue night. "Something's happened."

Some of the men jump out of bed with determination, inquisitiveness. Others stagger like mummies, shambling and mumbling, with impossibly itchy bellies. "What is it?" they ask. It's too late and too early for questions.

"It looks like that apartment building down the street," the women say. It's the sight of men and women, partially dressed, standing at their bedroom windows, strobe lights that fill them with both comfort and dread.

"It's probably just somebody speeding," the husbands say. The town is so small that one traffic violation brings out the entire force, curious like tomcats. It might not be anything at all.

He night is quiet, and above the songs of tree frogs, the couples can hear the opening and closing of cruiser doors, and the squawk of police radios, the murmur of voices with authority. "It's probably nothing," some of them say. "Come back to bed."

Some men, older, with bellies round and mustaches full and thick, wander over to the scene. They want to know what's going on. It's the kind of town where the police men have first names and the men in town call them by them. "What's going on, Bill?" the men ask.

Bill tips his cap. "Between you and me," he says. "I really

shouldn't be saying anything."

It's so late or so early that many people just stay up. "Have to get up in a few hours anyway," they reason. They go to the kitchen, they make coffee. Those with children check their beds.

Soon many of them are out on the corner. A group, an organized party, women in nightgowns and bathrobes and men in boxer shorts and sweatpants. "Bill says it's murder," they say. "Over by that apartment building."

Eventually the chief comes. He looks bleary, sad-eyed, tired. His hair looks slept on, even under his hat. His face, grey with stubble looks sick. "Lou," the men say. "Lou, what's going on?"

Lou makes his lips small, he raises his hands. "C'mon, people," he says, "go back to your homes."

Some of the younger couples, or those without children, listen. They look at each other and turn away. Some stay. "Lou, Lou, hey, Lou," they say. The chief waves them off. "Please. Go back to your homes." And eventually, in pairs, they do.

In the morning, only hours later, but seemingly a whole other day, cars pull out of driveways, pass slowly by the scene of the crime, the yellow police tape. They crane their heads. They want to know. But it's time to go to work.

Some of the older men are retired. They stand out with the young mothers and fathers who wait with their children at the bus stop. "Bill told me it was two guys from out of town," they say. "It was over that woman who lives there." The younger men nod their heads. They know that woman. They know why two men from out of town would fight and die for her. They hold their children's heads against their legs, stroke their hair. The children are not listening. They have no need for grown-up talk.

A lot of the younger couples, who live in the newer, bigger houses on the street, work from home. They all have dogs to walk. The dogs, the schnauzers and bichons and Russell terriers, strain at their leashes, furiously examine the crime scene. There are things they want to know. The men, young adults really, dressed up in designer sweats, reading news on their Blackberries, pull them away, call their names and whistle. The dogs, too, understand what happened here.

It's all the high school kids can talk about. They whisper about it in class. They asks questions that nobody has the answers to, but people try anyways. "She was sleeping with both of them," some say. "So they stabbed each other."

"I heard one shot the other," another says.

"I live two houses away," the first claims. "I would've heard it if it was a gun."

"It was a knife."

One of the teachers lives in town, two streets away, his daughter is in eighth grade. He interrupts his lecture, knows what's on everybody's mind. "Let's just get this out in the open," he says. But the children quickly realize he knows even less than they do.

There is more interest than usual in the local paper. It sells out at the supermarket, and people who usually never go into the convenience store on the edge of town because it's run by Pakistanis, stop in, looking for news. "Fifty cents," the Pakistani tells them. They pay him with exact change. They need to know.

But so much is unknown and unknowable. It's a popular topic for the next few days, and the older folks enjoy speculating, but by the end of the week it is over. The ones who bring it up in polite conversation only succeed in derailing the discussion.

"Yeah, I haven't heard anything new," one of them says.

"We'll probably never know," another shrugs.

"Did anyone see the game last night?" someone asks.
Everyone nods.

Soon there are no more tree frogs. The older men, the ones who have mustaches, start hoisting themselves up ladders, balancing their guts on the rungs, putting in their storm windows. There's a real chill in the morning air now.

The football practice field is one street over, on Walnut, and each afternoon a series of whistles is blown, and men sit at their computer desks and talk to their bosses on headsets and they watch out their windows as the girls cross country team runs by, one by one in a row, stern in their determination. The men stop listening, stop talking, and catch themselves admiring their own reflections in the computer monitors.

Weekends come and smoke rises up from backyards. Flat bed trucks with names painted on the side line the street, and the boys who went to high school years ago, but lived on different streets, clean the yards of leaves and debris.

A couple of houses get new siding installed. "It's easier to manage and clean," they say. "Less to worry about." Some men restain and weatherproof the wood on their decks and patios. Something is coming, something their homes need protecting from.

Friday nights are football nights, but the mosquitoes here have been bad--a boy and a girl both died a few towns away--so the games are on Saturday afternoons now. Everyone is waiting for the first frost.

One night, someone coming home from a bar somewhere

is passing through town. He gets pulled over at the top of the street, and soon three cruisers are there. Blue lights flicker against bedroom walls, but the few who get up see it's just someone pulled over.

"God, don't the cops have anything better to do around here," the men say, rolled over on their sides.

Some women think they see the girl at the supermarket. They're not sure. They think she's the one. The men play dumb. How should they know what she looks like? Others say they heard she left town. That house is just a stopover for drifters. There's been a Room for Rent sign up there ever since I've lived here. Nobody stays very long. It probably wasn't her. She's probably gone.

The frost comes, and the men wake early to scrape off the windows of their cars and their wives' cars. Their breath hangs rich and thick, like cartoon thought balloons around their heads. But they're empty.

The frost comes, just in time for Homecoming. The stands are packed, with men and women who have come to watch their sons or their neighbors' sons play. They chatter and gossip and cheer and howl in unison. They watch the scoreboard and yell at the refs for bad calls and missed calls.

"What are you, blind? You can't even see what's going on right in front of you!" They yell at the refs, just men in striped shirts, from other towns, just trying to make a little extra money on the side.

"Open your eyes!"

There's a dance the next night, all the kids are going, it's good they still do that. Good clean fun. I don't know, have you seen the way some of them dance? At least they're being supervised.

The dance ends at 10:30, but it's only the freshmen and sophomores, those being picked up by their parents, who are still there when the principal flicks on the lights. The senior class officers already have their brooms, are already stacking chairs. The DJ is loading his speakers into the back of a van.

Near the outskirts of town, by the pond, cars are running with their brake lights off. Music and murmuring, exhaust rising. "C'mon. Juswanna," the boys say. "Jus touch it."

The girls are demure. "This is nice," they say. "Let's go slow."

"Juswanna," the boys repeat. "Don't worry. We're safe here."

"I don't know."

"C'mon," the boys say.

There are porch lights on all up and down the street. Nervous mothers and anxious fathers lie in bed, watching the shadows from the porch lights until they hear car doors slam, keys jangling, and the lights goes off, and then they sleep.

And they hear the cars roar off, cars filled with boys with hours left on their curfew, or no curfew at all, now driving towards nowhere in particular, erections tight up against the denim of their jeans. Some of them keep driving until they have crossed the town line. Let them cruise around over there. Let them cause their trouble someplace else.

GIRL IN THE TREE

Looking at the ground, the wind made trees' shadows appear like they were moving. He had called out sick from work again, although he felt fine, and took a walk in his backyard to smoke and feel like maybe he wasn't connected to anything.

He thought about his wife and his daughter, the job he hated and the boss who humiliated him, the pinkness of his lungs turning gray, and what shape shadow the smoke made on the ground as he blew it from his mouth. For a moment, he felt like a dragon.

"Hello?" a voice, feminine and deep, girlish and rich, sounded from above. He dropped his cigarette in surprise, and looked around, turning on his heels unsteadily.

"Up here," the voice said again. He looked up in the trees. The sun was shining so brightly that he could only make out silhouettes. But it seemed there was a girl up in the tree.

"Hello?" he repeatedly cautiously.

The voice giggled, and though he tried to shield his eyes with his hands, he still couldn't see anything, or much of anything.

"My name is Tom," he said. It made sense to introduce himself. "What are you doing up there?"

"What are you doing down there?" she asked.

Tom spun around slowly, hoping a change in perspective would make her visible. But the sun was still so bright, and while he could see the silhouette of something up there in the trees, he couldn't be certain what it was.

"I don't know," he said.

Allison had come home on her lunch break and saw that her husband's car was still in the driveway. She looked through the house for him, and thought she saw him as she looked out the kitchen window.

"Tom?" she yelled from the back deck. "What are you doing? Who are you talking to?"

Allison's voice startled him, and he actually stumbled a bit as he turned and fell backwards, catching himself with one hand behind his back.

His wife ran out into the backyard, calling his name. He felt dizzy, and found that he hated the sound of his wife's voice calling his name. She said it again and again. "Tom? Tom?"

She seemed disappointed that he'd called out sick again, but squeezed his hand as she said, "I know you hate it. You'll find something soon." She smiled, and kissed the top of his hand. "I can feel it."

Tom told her he needed to lie down.

There was dinner and TV and tucking in and polite, pleasant sex, and when Allison awoke in the middle of the night, Tom was missing. She waited a half hour and then went looking. She saw a shadowy figure out in the backyard. Was it her husband? A prowler? Some kind of sex offender? Who was this strange man outside her house? She called his name.

"Tom?"

The figure in the shadows turned at this, and began walking back towards the house. Allison stood on the back porch in her nightgown, her hand on the automatic lighter left out by the grill.

Tom stepped into the porch light, uncertain and shuffling, his eyes red and swollen.

"It's the middle of the night!" she whisper-yelled. "What the hell are you doing?"

"I don't know," he replied. "Now it's too dark."

Emily had started kindergarten and Allison waited at the

bus stop with her daughter, along with all the other mothers and their sons and daughters.

"My daddy thinks there's a lady living in our woods," Emily said.

"What?" one mother said.

"Is it one of those environmentalists?" another asked Allison.

Allison shook her head and smiled, whispering to them in confidentiality "Tom goes out back to sneak cigarettes." She felt pleased with this. "He doesn't want Emily to know."

There was relief. Ralph smoked cigars in his game room, someone said, the upholstery up there is foul. At least Tom goes outside. And away from Emily. Ah, married life.

After school, Allison was short with her daughter, and Emily was given a time out after she spilled grape juice on the kitchen floor. It was an accident, Emily cried.

Don't tell me about accidents, Allison said gruffly, wiping the kitchen floor. The juice got lighter in color as it spread across the tiles. That means something, Allison thought. Then she sighed, told Emily to go on time out, and then finished wiping it up.

Emily was quiet and seemed to cry easily when Tom came home. He knew he shouldn't go out into the woods anymore. It was upsetting his family. That night when he took the dogs for a walk, he made sure to walk out in front of the house and to stop and talk to some of the neighbors. He hadn't been watching the Red Sox, and he didn't know any of the neighborhood children's names, but he was able to follow along enough that nobody knew there was anything wrong with him.

But something was wrong with him. He knew it deep

inside, in a place he knew he couldn't name. He woke up in the middle of the night from beautiful dreams and then stayed awake consumed by fears and anxieties. He wasn't who he said he was, all those years ago. He had always been someone else.

"I don't know what you're going through," Allison told him, rubbing his back, "but I want you to know that I'm here for you." Somehow that made everything worse.

He was spoken to at the gym for staring at the young women who were working out, but Tom had also been staring at the elderly men, too, fascinated by the sinew and muscles he knew somehow rested under their wrinkled and weathered skin. He was taking more cigarette breaks at work, and would often leave for lunch and never come back. But he stayed out of his woods.

One afternoon he left his car in his office parking lot and walked home. It was about 12 miles, and his shoes weren't cut out for it, and he started getting blisters on his heels, and the backs of his ankles started bleeding through his socks. Each step hurt and he stopped about halfway home at a public library two towns over. It was already starting to get dark, and he was surprised to find the library still open. When was the last time you even went to the library? he thought to himself. When was the last time you even read a book?

The woman at the circulation desk smiled at him when he walked in. "Are you here for the art show?" she asked. Tom saw no reason to say no. "I don't know who's left, but it's right through that door on the left," she said.

Tom draped his jacket over his forearm, and he had sweat through his shirtsleeves. As he walked around the tiny gallery room, he looked at each painting with a careless eye. He walked quickly around and looked at each of the paintings, unable to linger on any one too long. He couldn't even remember the last time he'd gone to a museum, and wasn't even sure what to look for in good art. He didn't know what he liked or disliked. He closed his eyes for a long moment, hoping that when he reopened them he would be able to see the things he was unable to see, the things he had been missing.

He looked again at the painting in front of him. It was a seascape, a harbor or a bay, and atop the curve of beach on a cliff was a large patch of woods. He stared intently on that tiny forest, and the closer and deeper he gazed, the less like trees it looked. It wasn't a forest at all. Just green marks of oil paint against brown, the impression of trees. He took a few steps back, but he couldn't see the trees anymore now that he had unseen them.

At the end of the gallery was a self-portrait of the artist, a young woman. In the painting, she faced away, looking off at something that Tom could not see. He had so many questions for her, but she had already turned away.

He felt like crying. He kept chewing his fingers and licking his lips, and he felt so salty, like he had been adrift at sea. He called Allison and she came and picked him up. Emily was asleep in the back.

"I think I'm going crazy," he told his wife.

"Oh, baby," she said. "It's okay. Just don't scare me like that again." But it was Tom who was scared. He had never felt so scared in his life. How could he stop scaring his wife when he couldn't stop scaring himself?

He carried his beautiful daughter from the car back into her bed. It was late, and he come such a long way and wanted to be carried himself. But these are the jobs we elect for ourselves when we have children, to carry them into their beds with our sore arms.

Emily stirred. "Daddy?"

"Hey, sweetie," he whispered.

"Where were you? I missed you."

"I got kind of lost coming home," he said.

She closed her eyes a bit. "I've seen her, too," she said.

"What?"

"I've seen her, too," she repeated, a whisper, a sigh.

There were raindrops on the roof. They padded down on the house and Tom wept openly at how little he had done to earn such faith.

The light from his bedroom sliced through the dark hallway. He stood at the ajar door and pushed it open slowly, afraid of what he might find. Allison was lying on her side, her two hands resting under her head.

"Allison," he said.

"Turn out the light," she murmured.

"I don't know if I can--" he said.

"Come to bed."

The following morning, they went to Emily's school. Columbus Day was approaching, and her class was perform-ing a play about the discovery of America. It was simplified kiddie stuff and it did little to correct the Eurocentric view of American history. You can't pretend you discovered something just because it's the first time you've seen it, Tom thought. He was still sore form the previous day's journey, and he shuffled uncomfortably in the hard wooden seats. Allison touched his leg and said, "Shh. Just enjoy the play."

He took a deep breath and tried to relax. He realized there was still a brokenness inside him, perhaps one that had always been there. So he sat, patiently, and listened as his daughter

{57}

and her friends explained that long ago, the very land we are standing on was nothing but forest, for miles in every direction, as far as the eye could see.

MEET THE FLINTSTONES

Look at them fall. They're little Technicolor snowflakes, first red, then green, then impossibly blue. I'm on my back; I'm laid low. There are things going on in my body, in my brain; there is blood rushing to all the wrong places and I know time is short. But there's something beautiful in the way these little sugared flakes of rice and grain, these little bits of the cereal we keep for our granddaughter, there's something beautiful in the way they fall, collect on my face and chest, beautiful and comical and tragic.

I thought I'd be more scared. I wake up each morning with strange aches, I fill the toilet with piss that stops and starts. I watch the mirror and see the boy, the man, I once was surrounded by old. I think about death daily, and any man my age tells you differently is lying. We trim our beards into neat little goatees, we wear our hair short and close to the scalp rather than watch it thin. We pedal our stationary bikes, jog by the pretty young wives in the neighborhood in our cut-off t-shirts, sweat forming little triangles on our chests, where our crucifixes sit. We eat green salads for lunch, we drink less beer than we'd like. Anything to not become old men like our fathers and grandfathers were. We'll never walk as slow, as unsteady as them. But we are aware. We are all aware that we will soon be dead like them. And I am scared, but not of what I'd thought I'd be. I woke up this morning, my back twitching, little spasms of sharp sore pain, gnawing against itself in the early morning light. Marsha's back was turned to me, wrapped in blankets like an Indian baby. She farted brightly and loudly through her slumber, did not stir.

The sun had risen, but not yet above the trees. The morning light was pale and gray as I made my way down to the kitchen. The hallway is lined with photographs of our daughter, high school portraits, middle, elementary, infant, traveling backwards through time. I wish now I had taken a second to look at them one last time. I will never see them, or her, again.

I'm not being melodramatic. There is something animal inside me that tells me that the light, the light, the spark inside me, is growing low. I know this, somehow. I know that the spark that lights my days is fading. I won't be making it through this.

I had wanted something sweet. I thought about dry toast or white egg omelettes that Marsha makes me eat, but I wanted something sweet. We keep the Fruity Pebbles and the Hydrox cookies for Megan, when she stays over. They're not for me, and I know that Marsha would be annoyed if she saw me stealing a bowl of our granddaughter's cereal. But I wanted something sweet.

Megan cries so easily. She stomps around our house, looking for her mother or for something else that isn't here, and she reaches up for me, and I can't help but pick her up each time. She rubs her red eyes with her tiny hands and she calls me a name that isn't mine, but I answer to it, I tell her, it's okay, Papa's here. I give her sweets and I hold her with one arm while I do my business around the house, until she falls asleep in my arm, rests her impossibly soft head against the hard part of my shoulder. Who is there now to carry her?

At first I thought it was my back when I fell over. I slid down, knocking over the cereal box on its side, grasping for something to catch myself. There goes my damn back, I thought. But it wasn't. It wasn't that at all. And as I lay on my back, realizing that it was something else, something bad, something I might not get up from, I looked up at the over-turned box as it balanced over the edge of the counter. And I saw, Hey look, it's Fred Flintstone.

And suddenly I'm a boy again, laid out in front of my parents' old Magnavox, resting on my hip, my hands under my head, like an Egyptian princess. I don't get the jokes. The whole thing makes perfect sense to me. Cars with no bottoms that you power by running your feet along the ground. Wooly mammoths blowing water out of their trunks as showers. Pre-historic birds whose beaks are turntable needles. It all seems so real. So logical.

In the far corner of the room is my sister. She's humming a little song to herself, brushing the hair of her doll, pretending its her child, and she sings to it, combs its hair, loves it like we do the things we really love. Lizzie, quiet down, I'm watching TV. She's quiet now forever. Cancer took her eight or nine or ten years ago. Marsha held my hand as I looked into her casket, as I prepared to bury the last member of my family. I didn't cry then. I had buried my mother and then my father and now my sister, but I didn't cry. But thinking about that morning, thinking about that doll and that song that existed only then in that moment and never again. Christ, I'm crying now. I'm crying now.

They've stopped falling, and the ones that have pooled on my chest slide off and make this noise against the tile floor. It seems so loud. I hope it doesn't wake Marsha. Fat, stinky Mar-sha still sleeping, still safe. I resent her sometimes for not being the girl I married; for losing light and gaining weight, for getting tired early, for sleeping in late. But I also love her for it, too. I love her for letting herself become imperfect in front of me, for trusting me and having faith that I would accept it.

There are days where we barely speak to one another, where she leaves for work and I go down into my workshop, I cook dinner and leave it for her while I go to the gym. I love her for allowing that silence, for nurturing it with me like it was our child, for giving it the space it needed to grow and mature.

We lost a child once, after Lauren. We hadn't much time with it, time to think of names or imagine futures for it. It was an idea, planted inside her, that never got a chance to fully take root. I dreamt for a while afterwards that it was still inside her, months, years after it had flushed itself out of her, aware before we were of how impossible its life was to be. In my dreams, I would it imagine it still there, just waiting for the right time to be born. But there is no right time to be born, anymore than there is a right time to die.

God, don't let Marsha find me. Let her keep sleeping forever.

I never wanted to think I would be in this position, facing death flat on my back. I never thought I would have the chance--I would die in my sleep, I would be taken instantly from a heart attack--and I never thought I would have the chance to ask God why he gives us this light, this spark of life, only to snuff it out. There is still more to do. I can feel the cool tile floor against my cheek and know that beneath it, down in my workshop is the dollhouse I've been working on for Megan. I haven't been using the workshop much in the last ten years. When I was younger, I used to make birdhouses and little wooden coathooks for friends and neighbors. I would spend hours down in my workshop, hammering and sawing and sanding, never charging anybody anything more than materials. I stopped it when Lauren got into high school, and things around here tightened up. Everybody I knew had a birdhouse, and I never had much interest in trying to sell them. So the workshop collected dust, became the room we put the old furniture we didn't want anymore, the old lamps and broken appliances, the things we never had the heart or the energy to throw out.

But I've been down there recently now, building a dollhouse for my granddaughter, but it's cruelly so unfinished. It's not even close to being done. If they ever go down there and find it, I don't know if they'll even be able to tell what it was I was making. I had just started it. That's what's so unfair. I was using my hands again, Lord. I was building, building things to make my daughter and my granddaughter happy. Where is the fairness in taking me away with so much left undone?

My daughter lost her job recently. Times are tight everywhere. But she's such a good person, better than her mother or me, and I worry what this will do to her. I feel myself fading so fast, and my thoughts are about Lauren and the checks I've given her these past few months, and how she cries each time I give her one. Take it, I say. Think of Megan. I don't mean to cry, she'll tell me. I just wish this was easier.

If it was easier, it wouldn't be life. It's like something my mother would've said to me. There's something true to it. God, I love her so much. I don't even know if I know how much I love the person she is, who I picked up and swung by her arms and Marsha would worry that I'd pull them right out of the sockets. But she squealed so, such moments of joy. They're what we live for, aren't they? And I want to protect her from all the hurt and the pain, let her have a life full of only joy. But that isn't really the point, is it?

What is the point then? What is the point of living a good life, of eating right and being kind and dying on your back one morning, covered in Fruity Pebbles. Someone will have to clean up this mess.

There are dogs barking somewhere. Maybe they know. Maybe they can smell it or sense it, whatever it is. Maybe they feel it hovering.

I am able to look above me through the window. The sun is starting to burn atop the trees. I watch it through my teary eyes. I watch it forever, and I think that's it. I think about the sun and the cartoon caveman above me and it all make sense. The flame, the light, the fire we weren't given it by Prometheus, or by some God. We make it ourselves by striking against the sharp and hard parts of life. That's how we make the spark. That's how we build our fires.

But mine is quickly dying. I wish I could write some of this down for my wife, my daughter, my granddaughter. I'd say, it's okay, my loves. I know that life seems terrible and horrible and unfair. I know my leaving makes our small family that much smaller. I know you don't think you can handle it. I used to think that way. I used to think we were all so soft, so delicate, so fragile that we needed to be sheltered and protected. But we all, each of us, we are all made of much tougher stuff.

ABOUT (2)

I feel I should mention the young artist whose artwork graces both the cover and the inside illustrations of this book. It has to do with Jeff Kent again.

The first summer I came back to the summer program, the first summer I was Jeff Kent's intern, I met Kristin Texeira. She was only a tenth grader back then, and would probably be as embarrassed to see her tenth grade self as I would be to see mine. She wasn't a particularly exemplary pupil the first couple of weeks--I knew her more from our interactions on campus outside the classroom then from anything she did in class. But one day, Jeff Kent gave the students time in class to write and my job was to circulate around the library in which the students had spread themselves out and check on their progress. I popped over to visit with Kristin and she showed me what she had started writing.

It was good. I liked it. I told her that, and I told her to keep working on it. It was the story of going to visit a senior center when she was a small child and watching one of the residents perform simple magic tricks. It surprised me, something that is difficult to do to someone who has read as much as I have. She continued working on it during the entire class period. I watched her write it. There was something electrifying about watching someone discover her voice over the course of an hour and fifteen minutes, but with a little tweaking overnight, Kristin had written a wonderful piece. It's a piece I still use each summer as an example in my classes.

As I mentioned before, the summer I lost my job, I had

decided to use the opportunity unemployment had presented me to attempt to become a writer again. I began writing stories again as a testing ground. I was able to write a few stories and complete them (I often wonder how many partially completed stories and novels there are floating around the world on hard-drives and in file drawers) but they were more like puzzles than stories. I just started with the edge pieces and worked my way in.

The first story I started writing that didn't feel that way was the collection's title story "Girl in the Tree." I had started with the edge pieces, and when I got to a certain point I didn't want to just fill in the rest. The story wanted to go somewhere else. I had been writing in a local park, and I decided to put the story aside and take a walk and clear my mind, try and figure out how to move the story along. I also had to pee. So I walked to the only place I could think of with a restroom open to the public: the local library.

After I had evacuated my bladder, I walked around the library in an attempt to look like an actual library patron. Near the front lobby they had set aside an area for local artists' work. I looked at each painting, and when I saw one--a portrait of a young woman from the back--the whole rest of the story appeared in my head. I can't really explain the train of thought clearly any more than I can recount each step I took this morning since I woke up. It all happened so fast. The story was there, and I stared at the painting a little longer. There was a placard on the wall with the artist's name. It was Kristin Texeira.

At the time, I lived in a small town surrounded by other small towns. It isn't a totally amazing thing that I would wander into a former student's art display one town over. What is amazing is that while I had been there when Kristin had discovered her voice five years earlier, in a way, she was there when I had rediscovered my own.

This is one of those lame stories that writers tell. It's 100% true, and this collection exists just as much to showcase Kristin's artwork as it does to provide a home for these stories. Maybe even more so.

-Ryan J. Tressel
Somewhere on the Back River
September 2010

Other books by
Ryan J. Tressel

The While

Immortallo

more information available at:
www.ryantressel.com

Lots of people read these stories in various forms, and for that I am grateful.

Darrell Morey, Jesse Thomas, Anna Gregoline,
David R. Surette, Autumn Alden
and Lisa DeLorenzo

And as always, big big thanks to
Katie Rosenberg

-RJT

Proof

Made in the USA
Charleston, SC
19 October 2010